# JOEY ON HIS OWN

## Eleanor Schick

THE DIAL PRESS  NEW YORK

Published by
The Dial Press
1 Dag Hammarskjold Plaza
New York, New York 10017

Library of Congress Cataloging in Publication Data
Schick, Eleanor, 1942–     Joey on his own.
*Summary:* Joey goes shopping by himself
for the first time when his mother sends him out
to buy a loaf of bread.
[1. Shopping—Fiction.] I. Title.
PZ7.S3445Jo  [E]   81-68770   AACR2
ISBN 0-8037-4302-5 (lib. bdg.)
ISBN 0-8037-4301-7 (pbk.)

The art for each picture consists of a pencil drawing
with two color overlays, all reproduced as halftone.

Reading Level 2.2

*For Jeremy*

# CONTENTS

# 1

## NO BREAD

One Saturday
my mother opened the breadbox
to make sandwiches for lunch,
and there was no more bread.

She said, "Someone will have to
go to the store to buy bread,
or we won't have any lunch.

"I can't go out today.
Jill has a fever
and the doctor said
she must stay home
until she gets well.

"Joey, you're old enough now
to go to the store by yourself.

"I think you should be the one
to buy the bread."

Mom took the last piece of bread
out of the bag.

She said, "Buy the kind of bread
that comes in this bag.
It's the one we all like best.

"You can go to the store
around the corner
where we always do our shopping."
Then she took out her purse
and gave me the money.
"Keep this in your pocket
until you give it to the lady
at the checkout line."

She handed me my jacket,
my mittens, and my hat.

And she didn't even give me
a chance to say no.

# 2

## THE STREET

Going downstairs alone is easy.
I've done this before.
Sometimes I go to Jerry's house
after school.

And I go downstairs by myself
when I get the mail
from the mailbox.
I even have the key.

But I've never gone shopping

without Mom before.

The buildings on our street

look taller than they ever did.

The traffic sounds noisier.

The mean kid

who lives down the street

looks meaner.

I walk past him quickly.

I pretend I don't see him.

I don't even give him

a chance to be mean.

The dog behind the gate

barks louder today.

And the store

around the corner

seems so far away.

# THE STORE

The store
looks bigger and more crowded
than it does when I go with Mom.
I guess everyone
likes to do their shopping
on Saturday.

I can't even find the bread.

A man with a white apron on

asks me if I need help.

I ask him where the bread is.

He tells me how to find it.

Then he says,

"You're very grown-up

to be buying bread

all by yourself."

I find the place where the bread is,
but it looks like there are
at least a hundred kinds.

I take out the bread bag
that Mom gave me.

There is a lady

who is buying bread too.

She stops and says,

"That's the kind of bread

I'm looking for.

They keep it right here."

We get our bread together.

The lady says, "It's fresh,

because they just delivered it

this morning."

She says, "Now I have to buy

some milk and eggs."

I thank her for helping me.

I take my bread

to the front of the store.

That's where the checkout lines are.
I find the shortest line.

In front of me

a baby in a shopping cart

is eating pretzels.

I make funny faces
and the baby laughs
while we wait on line.
That makes her mother happy.

When it's my turn,

the checkout lady takes my bread.

She presses the keys

on the cash register

to show how much it costs.

I give her the money

that I kept in my pocket.

She gives me the change

and puts the bread

in a brown paper bag.

The lady says,

"Thank you very much, sir.

Good-bye now, and have a nice day!"

# 4

## BRINGING HOME
## THE BREAD

I feel terrific!

I did everything my mother told me.

The corner isn't

far away at all.

The dog behind the gate

isn't even barking.

He's just sleeping in the sun.

The mean kid can see
that I don't care how mean he is.
He thinks I don't see him,
and that's just what I want.

The traffic is making
the same loud noises,
and I like the sounds.

The buildings are just high enough
to keep the sun
from shining in my eyes.

I check the mailbox
and the mail has come.
Mom will be glad
when I bring it upstairs.

I ring the bell three times
so she'll know it's me.

Mom opens the door.

She's happy when I give her the mail.

Then I give her the brown bag.

She opens it and finds the bread.

"It's just the right kind!" she says.

I give her the change

that I kept in my pocket.

She says, "You did a perfect job!"

Mom takes the bread into the kitchen.
"Jill had some soup for lunch,
and now she's sleeping." Mom says.
"Our soup and sandwiches
will be ready in two minutes."

Boy, I'm hungry!

I don't think I can wait!

I take off my jacket

and my mittens and my hat.

I hang them up.

Mom calls, "Lunch is ready!"

And it never tasted so good!